What do you say when somebody asks where are you coming from? Here is the response of Georgia O'Keeffe (1887–1986) who found her home in New Mexico after a long journey:

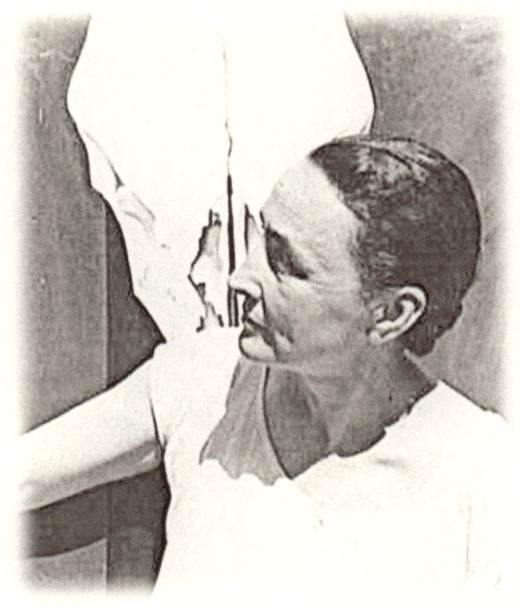

"Where I was born and where and how I have lived is unimportant.
It is what I have done with where I have been that should be of interest."

Santa Fe Voices

Poems of New Mexico

Charles Sullivan

Contents

Santa Fe
Voices

ADVOCATE

I have little enough
to say for myself,
yet my mouth is busy
pleading for those
whose tongues are tied.

Now and then I listen.

Now and then my thoughts
drift away like the smoke
from a smothered fire
while other people choke,
while other people weep.

ARTIST IN RESIDENCE

I saw two rainbows today.

The first was something
I might have done:

hazy strokes and faint gray arcs,
then pigments blending together
in masterful, subtle ways
as the sun burned through
its cloud cover.

The second one was clearly
the work of a beginner.

BEAR TALK

You've been sprawling
on these matted weeds and grasses
near the river. And I can tell
what you've been eating here,
elderberries and horsetails
and green apples gone wild,
and anything slower than you
that was moving on four legs.
You're busy building fat, like me,
before you go back into the hills
to hibernate. I know this
without words. Today I seem
to be some kind of a bear myself,
not as broad or heavy as your tracks
say you are, but fiercer I hope,
in case we ever meet.

BIBLE STUDIES

At the orphanage in Oklahoma
they weren't about to tell you
what they thought you were
or where you might've come from.

If you didn't know the words
of their prayers and hymns,
they made you study after school
in empty rooms with maps to pull down.
You could look at any country
and pretend. I usually picked China
because it was far away.

When I drew pictures of dragons in the back
of my Bible, I got punished. But later they found
a much bigger dragon on the blackboard, with claws
to grip the ground, and real wings, and breath stinking
of dead things, and squinty eyes that said
I'm trouble, man. . .

you better not mess with me.

BLESSINGS

The priest is gone, with his *botija*
of holy water, and 'most everyone else
has found a place to sit down, ready
for this meal we're serving,

but my cousin Elbert is still outside
in the dark somewhere, burying
the fetishes he brought from home
to bless our marriage:

badger to give us independence;
wolf to help us know our path;
mountain lion to get us moving;
and bear to keep us going,
no matter how hard things are.

What a good way for us
to start life's journey together,
my wife and me.

BLUE BAYOU

Saturday night
at the RV park
there's music playing
loud enough to rock
a bikers' moon.

I try to sing along,
except for some high notes—
but the neighbor's dogs are saying
they don't know this tune
and they don't like it.

CAUGHT IN THE MIDDLE

My sister says
the gas is half empty,
my brother-in-law says
no, it's half full,
and I'm sitting here
between them, hoping
he's right for once,
because he spent
his last twenty bucks
before we left the rodeo,
buying her a cowboy hat
I knew she wouldn't wear.

COMING TO YOUR SENSES

You've walked far enough with me.
Now turn back and see the canyon
for what it is: just one of many
such places, nothing remarkable about it,
except the stream that seldom fails
and those caves high on the north wall,
under the rim. Maybe you heard
something there, saw something.
Maybe you didn't. Turn back now,
please, listen to the water flowing,
watch the play of light. Rub your hands
with pine needles. That's right,
sniff your fingers. Get the feel
of the trees.

DESCRIBING HIS WIFE

She seemed dark enough when I met her,
the young man said. Hands as rough
as mine from cleaning houses, that first
winter between jobs. So I took her out
a few times, movies, pizza, no big deal.

When things got a little better for us
and she began to let me see more of her,
I was almost frightened by how white
she looked; you understand what I mean?
Yet there was something about her.

Then one night she kissed me, led me
upstairs in this place she was renting.
Her face, her arms, her legs were paler
than the peeled birch rails of the bed.
Whatever it may have been that made her
different, I felt like I was at home.

DOUBLE OR NOTHING

The only charm I ever wanted
to carry around in my pocket
was a two-headed raven,
black as jet, that belonged
to my mother's uncle, Freddie.
He was said to be harmless
though often in trouble.

"Why do you need this old thing?"
he'd tease me.

"Same reason you needed it,
Freddie," I'd tell him now
if he could hear me. Him
and his double.

DOUSING FOR WATER

Letting my mind wander,
letting my feet go left or right,
while holding this forked twig
loosely in both hands. . . .

Did I say willow? That's for finding
where you should dig if you live
out in the desert. Here in town
I could trace a buried water pipe
with almost any kind of stick;
my father liked to try it barefoot
with two steel rods crossing each other.

He had nothing against wood,
that I know of, but he was
mostly a welder by trade,
he felt better with the metal
warming his fingers.

DREAM CATCHER

My son will see to it
that his son never wants
for anything as he grows up.

What's left for me to do?

I could tell him my stories
a few more times. I could
shuffle through the steps
my own father taught me,
singing the songs of hunter
and prey. I could stay awake
at night, catching a little boy's
dreams, letting only the best ones
descend upon him gently, gently
as feathers from the gods.

EPITAPH FOR A WIDOW

She couldn't get over
the loss; every morning
after church she'd be out
working on something
as he would have done,

scraping the dusty road
with his tractor
or plowing a field
he had no water for,

whatever it took
to show the earth
who's boss.

EYE CONTACT

Tough guys?
I don't look them
in the eye any more.
I see right through them
just as they see life
and death through me.

THE FASTEST RUNNER IN THE WORLD

My father never tired of telling me
how fast he could run when he was my age,
growing up in Texas border towns
where they didn't have track meets
and they didn't give you prizes.

I'm not half the runner he was,
but I can move a lot faster,
and I've got medals from Afghanistan
to prove it. Yesterday I did a mile
in less than four minutes, today
or tomorrow I'm going to break three,
I'm on a roll. The trick is
to keep your feet from touching
the ground, which is easy
if you have no legs.

FESTIVAL AT SAN ILDEFONSO

When I was a child standing
close to my father and mother,
watching the dancers come
into the square, I thought
they were deer dressed as people,
I wondered how they could wear
shoes like ours on their feet,
moving so lightly, and never
stumble, with the drums beating
faster and faster. Even now,
years later, holding the hands
of my two youngest, something
makes me hesitate to say
that people do this dancing
dressed as deer.

FURNITURE MAKER

Not fired, not tired,
I just don't feel
like working any more.

I'll sit here looking
at this piece of cottonwood.

Maybe see a saint to carve
before I give my tools away
to someone who could use them.

GARDEN TO GARDEN

People down here
have been waiting all winter
for snow to melt up there
in the mountain passes,

for streams to flow again
and irrigation ditches.

Before the first of April
they'll clear out the *acequias*
which their ancestors dug
from one place to the next,
from garden to garden,
so that water may be shared
as freely as it was
in the old days.

HANDY WOMAN

It's harder for me
to fix things
than it used to be
when I was young.

I can still see
pretty good, but this
new hammer keeps missing
the nails, and the nails
aren't worthy of the wood.

HEARSAY

You say there are people like us
living beyond the mountains?
I doubt it. And what would I do
if I didn't? I'm not going to go
looking for them; I've got plenty
of hard-up friends and poor relations
already. And I sure don't need
to find another me! Years ago
it might have been different.
I remember hearing stories
about some magic lake, deep
and windless, where you could see
your own twin if you'd been good.
I was only a kid, I believed all that
for a while, after my friend Carlos
ran away. I almost went looking.

HORSE DOCTOR

What's my formula
for success?

I don't talk to horses
and they don't talk to me.

It's that simple.

JAIL BREAK

Around midnight the gates
are unlocked for a while,
so I can get up if I wish to,
stretch my legs, walk right
out of my cell, walk as far
as the end of this building,
where they have windows,
and see how much snow is left
on the peaks of the mountains,

though lately what I take to be
snow turns out to be moonlight,

or it could be moonlight reflected
by clouds, the more I think about it.

LEARNING LATIN

Sister calls this stuff
a dead language. So why
should we waste our time?

I am, you are, he is.

She's making us learn
what the old words mean
before she'll let us sing them
at mass.

I am, you are, he is.

The other kids will do it
if I do.

MAN WITH GUITAR

Hang a bunch of chili peppers
over your stove, don't expect me
to eat them. Bring the famous
cello player here for a day,
don't invite me to meet him.

And who am I? Two clues.

I'm the fool who's getting high
on songs nobody sings.

I'm so cool the sun can't melt
my wax and feather wings.

MAN WITHOUT GUITAR

Ran out of gas
as I sometimes do,
and couldn't find
but a dollar forty
under the seat,

nickels and dimes
and three of those new
galvanized quarters,

so I'm walking home
with holes in my boots
and it's starting to rain
as it sometimes does,
drops of different sizes
like small change.

MEXICAN HISTORY

Our "man of the people"
must have had three faces:

one for us, one for those
he served, and one for the *pesos*
that will never be minted.

OLD MAN LIVING ON CERRO GORDO

I measure these hills each year,
like children, and mark the frame
of my door with a pencil.
See here? They are growing taller.
Or maybe I'm stooping more.

No matter.

They are home to the spirits
that will come for me one day.
I am not unimportant. I have
friends in high places.

PARKING LOT

You people coming
out of the movies,
talking and laughing,
what have you seen
that's so amusing?

Some of you notice me
freezing in my rusty car
with the window broken,
no heat: do I look like
a monster or a freak?

If I hadn't used my money
for other things tonight,
I could be walking with you
now, and believe me—nobody
would know the difference.

PAWN SILVER

I've handed over
everything else I own
one piece at a time:
my mother's bracelets,
my father's hatband,
her rosary, his spurs.

All I've got left
is this belt buckle,
mister. I use it
to hold my pants up,
but if you need it
worse than I do, well,
let me take two or three
turns of your heavy twine,
plus canned goods to last
'til the end of the month,
and help me figure out
what I still owe you.

PEDRO & ROSALITA

Pedro's been acting
kind of strange lately,
calling his pickup "Rosalita"
and clicking his tongue
as though he could help her
to make it up the long hills.

All she needs is just a kick
in the ass, if you ask me.

POKER FACE

House keeps dealing
cards like these,
I keep on betting
hand after hand.

You can't beat me.
I've got the rent
and the car payment
tucked in my shoe.

I'm no more hooked
than you might be,
whatever it is
you're playing at.

REVOLUTION

Next time around,
maybe we'll be the ones
to decide things
like the shape of the sky,
the colors of the hills;
maybe God will look down
at what we've tried to do
and sing our praises.

ROAD RUNNERS

The snake-eating roadrunner
is said to be our state bird.
Don't ask me why.

We've lived in New Mexico
for eight years on and off,
we haven't seen one yet.

All kinds of other creatures
out running the roads, though:
low riders and high riders
and some more or less
normal like us.

SAMBA LESSON

Put your arms around my neck,
yes, like that, then just let me
put my two hands on your waist,
like this, and before you know it
you're dancing the samba the way
the samba was meant to be danced.
You see? You've got natural rhythm,
your body makes the moves better
than I do already. You don't need
a teacher. And I hope you're not
getting embarrassed about how good
it feels. Why don't you look at
something over my shoulder, try
to think about somebody else, maybe
a husband who'd rather stay home?

I won't say another word—your hips
can do the talking for both of us.

SECRETS

I used to be so ashamed
of my secret thoughts.

I'd whisper them in those ruins
at the south edge of the mesa,
where the dead couldn't hear
my revelations.

Now I'm happy to be out walking
the streets of this town or any town
with living people in it, morning
noon or night, telling what little I know
and much I'm not sure of, to anyone
who'll listen.

SEEING THINGS

for Carlos Eldorado

You think you see
water in the desert
when you're thirsty,
or cities of gold
if you're broke.

I think I see
the signs my old one
spoke about, the scat
of hundreds of buffalo,
maybe more than he saw
as he smoked.

SHAPING CLAY

She talks to us
while making pottery
the simple way, shaping clay
with her fingers, waiting
patiently for summer sun
to dry it, to harden it,
then painting the design
she knows by heart.

Red, yellow, black.

People in a circle,
people in a line twisting
forward and back.

So the dance goes on,
though the dancers
are long gone.

SHOUTING TO THE CORN MAIDEN

Whenever we broke a plate,
a cup, a bowl, anything like that,
my grandmother would smash all
the pieces, then take them out back
and throw them into the corn
as far as she could, shouting
"Grow me some new dishes, you,
why don't you?"

After I was big enough to work,
I bought a whole set and hid them
where she'd be sure to find them.
They were just plastic, not the kind
she wanted, clay. But she reached up
and kissed me anyway.

SIGN LANGUAGE

The shaman said nothing
to me. He drew this figure
on a piece of hide.

If it means lightning
that's all right,
lightning doesn't scare me;
what's the worst thing
it could do?

If it's a snake
I'll find some way
to live with it, because
America's still a free country
and the snakes got here
before I did.

SITTING ON THE SIDEWALK

It's not you
I'm listening to,
I hear voices
from a better time
and place, but
I can tell what
you're saying
by the look
on your face,
I can read you
like a book
that people wouldn't buy
if you paid them.

SPOTTING SCOPE

A couple of inches
below the horizon,
half way down a hill,
three coyotes spot me
spotting them, hear me
not hearing them,
smell me not smelling
the hot stench of their kill.

STORY TELLER

A woman known as the story teller
has been living among us all winter,
offering youngsters and elders
her breast, leaving the rest of us
to do whatever must be done
to stay alive.

We hunt, we eat, we sleep,
we almost dream; the truth is
that nothing much happens.

THURSDAYS OFF

Once a week I'd go shopping down town
or just looking at dresses in store windows
if it was close to the end of the month.
Now if it's nice I sit on a bench
in the plaza. Save my money
and rest my ankles. Enjoy the music,
which is free, when they have any.
Lean back. Try not to close my eyes.

It's true what they say, though:
the sky is so blue around here
it makes you want to cry
about the place you grew up in,
and the clouds are whiter
than the sheets your mother washed
for other people's beds.

TOUGH LOVE

I don't feed my fetishes
the way some people do,
with little pinches
of corn meal or wheat
from a leather pouch.
I let them go hungry
like the rest of us.

I don't water things
except the rose we planted
outside the kitchen window
after my daughter died.
Anything else will make it
on its own. That's what
roots are for.

VILLAGE POLITICS

The owner of the grocery store came to see me. Mister Busy-Body is his name. "This village needs a new mayor," he said. "The job has been vacant since August 23rd of last year. It doesn't take much time, the way I see it, so it doesn't pay much."

"I'm no politician," I said.

"You're the fattest guy around," he said. "If there was ever any trouble about money or such things, you couldn't leave in a hurry."

"That figures," I said. "People aren't likely to trust a skinny guy."

"Not after the last one," he said.

"I'll think it over," I said, "I'll talk to my wife and get back to you. Soon as I finish my lunch."

WHAT'S NEW?

An orange cat,
four dogs, three humans
have sauntered past the open door
of my *casita* this morning.

Only the cat pauses to look in
at a stranger writing and talking
to himself, among stacks of books
and empty boxes.

WINTER IS WATER

Snow again last night.
Wet and heavy as I try
to shovel it. My hills
are covered with junipers
bending under the weight
of all this snow. I'm older
than the trees are, they get
no pity from me. I tell them
if they want water enough
for all to drink next summer,
they must bear the burden now.
Winter is water, I tell them.

WOMAN FROM ACOMA

In those days,
she said, our *pueblo*
was known as Sky City.

Every house on the mesa
had its own special ladder.

When warm weather came,
people would sit together
on the roofs late at night,
talking with neighbors,
reading the stars for news
or entertainment.

In those days the great
constellations had names,
personalities, and their stories
were constantly changing;
you couldn't just lie back
and go to sleep, thinking
"I've seen that one before."

WORKING LATE

The shadow of my hand
could be a bird in flight,
a *chacha-laca* or a shy
guanito by the size of it,

but then it's gone
and I'm still sitting here,
making little cages,

I'm cutting sticks
and knotting threads,
working late tonight
to earn my wages.

Notes on the Poems

These poems are meant to stand on their own, and most of them do, but some references may not be clear to all readers.

BLESSINGS: In New Mexico, "fetishes" are small animals carved in stone by Zuni Indians and others. Traditionally they were believed to impart specific powers to their keepers, as long as they were properly cared for and treated with respect.

BLUE BAYOU: The title refers to a song made famous by Roy Orbison during the 1960s. His distinctive "rockabilly" voice was silenced for years after his wife died in a motorcycle accident in 1966.

CAUGHT IN THE MIDDLE: Picture an older-model car or pickup truck, with three people riding side by side on the bench seat.

DOUBLE OR NOTHING: This two-headed bird is a particularly interesting example of a carved stone fetish or charm (see BLESSINGS above). If a single raven helps us to get comfortable with the inner, darker, less familiar aspects of ourselves, according to tradition, then what does a double signify?

OLD MAN LIVING ON CERRO GORDO: A natural feature called "Cerro Gordo" (Fat Hill) gives its name to one of the roads leading out of Santa Fe.

FESTIVAL AT SAN ILDEFONSO: The people of San Ildefonso Pueblo, New Mexico, still engage in ancient ceremonies and rituals, as well as tribal dances. Most of these events are closed, but San Ildefonso Feast Day is open to the public every January 23.

GARDEN TO GARDEN: The hand-dug irrigation ditches known as *"acequias"* have been used for hundreds of years in New Mexico and other dry lands. Water being so precious, they are carefully managed. Acequia water law requires that all persons with irrigation rights participate in ditch maintenance, including the annual springtime cleanup.

MAN WITH GUITAR: In Greek mythology, Daedalus was a creative person who escaped from prison by making wings of feathers and wax for himself and his son, Icarus. To the father's dismay, however, the boy flew too close to the sun, with disastrous results.

PAWN SILVER: In the old days, some people who lived near trading posts could survive by "pawning" or borrowing money on personal belongings such as jewelry hand-crafted of silver, turquoise, etc.

PEDRO & ROSALITA has no connection with Bruce Springsteen's song *Rosalita* (Come Out Tonight)" which seems to evoke New Jersey rather than New Mexico. Any resemblance is purely coincidental.

ROAD RUNNERS: These fast-moving birds do exist, whether we happen to notice them or not. "Low riders" are cars or trucks altered so that they barely clear the surface of the road, even when it's flat. "High riders" (usually pickup trucks with oversized wheels and tires) are just the opposite.

SHOUTING TO THE CORN MAIDEN: The Corn Maiden or someone like her can be found in the belief systems of various people, including the Hopi, Pueblo, and Zuni Indian tribes.

SIGN LANGUAGE: A shaman is a person supposed to have access to, and influence in, the world of spirits. Shamanic symbols used in pictographic art in New Mexico and elsewhere include the zigzag line, probably a reference to rain or lightning in places where rain is essential to survival.

STORY TELLER: Story telling occurs in families, tribes, communities the world over; in New Mexico the idea of doing this as a vocation is closely associated with some of the Pueblo people, who make elaborate clay figures of women, men, or even animals telling stories to attentive audiences.

TOUGH LOVE: Feeding fetishes is part of the tradition of taking care of them, in order to receive their benefits (see BLESSINGS above).

WOMAN FROM ACOMA: Sky City is one of three reservations making up Acoma Pueblo, about sixty miles west of Albuquerque. Sometimes called "the place that always was."

Acknowledgments & Credits

Most of these poems were inspired by people I encountered while living in New Mexico—people from every walk of life, who would not ordinarily give voice to poetry themselves. I have tried presumptuously to write for them. Thanks to Hugh Nissenson, the late Diane Middlebrook, and the legendary Carlos Eldorado, among others, for reading and commenting on some of the results. Earlier versions of several poems have appeared in *Poet Lore* ("Coming to Your Senses" and "Thursdays Off"), *The Harwood Anthology,* Albuquerque, NM ("Dousing for Water"), and a Web magazine called *Mnemosyne* ("Dream Catcher," "Secrets," "Sitting on the Sidewalk," and "Story Teller"). Prizes were awarded for "Shaping Clay" and "The Fastest Runner in the World" at poetry competitions in San Francisco and Oakland, CA.

Also included in some editions of this book are nine selections from *Uncle Sam's Family:* Stories of Exceptional Americans and Their Amazing Animals ("Cinderella of Santa Fe," "Elfrego Baca the Fearless Deputy," "Judge Roy Bean and His Pet Bear," "Pecos Bill Rides a Mountain Lion," "Black Bart the Stagecoach Robber," "Sweet Betsey from Pike," "Fur-Bearing Trout," "Jesse James Outsmarted," and "Wind-Wagon Thomas") copyright 2012 Charles Sullivan.

The cover image for *Santa Fe Voices* is an oil painting in the collection of the Smithsonian American Art Museum, Washington, DC, by William Penhallow Henderson (1877-1943) entitled "The Gossip," also known as "Two Women in Santa Fe." Gift of Arvin Gottlieb. Accession Number 1991.205.10. Used by permission. Thanks to Dr. Elizabeth Broun, Director of the Museum. All other images used in *Santa Fe Voices* are believed to be in the public domain, namely: photo of Georgia

O'Keeffe and drawing of howling coyote from wpclipart.com; drawing of bull skull from All-free-download.com; roadrunner photo from science4jengling.wordpress.com. The Georgia O'Keeffe quotation was found in "The Painter's Keys" (quote.robertgenn.com). Book cover design by Tatiana Vila. Book design by Maureen Cutajar, www.gopublished.com.

About the Author and His Other Books

Charles Sullivan, born in Massachusetts, has lived, studied, and worked in approximately 30 different U.S. zip codes, including Santa Fe, before settling down in California. He is the author and editor of numerous books for adults, teenagers, and younger children. Go to www.charlessullivanbooks.com for titles, descriptions, and book reviews. His other interests include history, education, public service, the environment, and boating. For further information about Sullivan's varied career, see *Who's Who in the World.*

His latest book is *Uncle Sam's Family: Stories of Exceptional Americans and Their Amazing Animals.* Published by Kezaco in 2012. Available in electronic (ebook) format at www.smashwords.com/books/view/269769. (ISBN-10: 0-985411-0-5; ISBN-13: 978-0-9855411-0-1). Also available as a paperback (POD) from Amazon.com (ISBN-10: 0-9855411-1-3; ISBN-13: 978-0-9855411-1-8).

Contents of *Uncle Sam's Family:* 44 lively American folktales including Black Bart the stagecoach robber, Br'er Rabbit outsmarting Br'er Fox, Casey Jones' train wreck, Crook-Jaw the whale, Daniel Boone, Jake Dorsey and his endless herd of horses,

UNCLE SAM'S FAMILY

STORIES OF EXCEPTIONAL AMERICANS AND THEIR AMAZING ANIMALS

CHARLES SULLIVAN

Frankie & Johnny, fishing for fur-bearing trout, George Washington and the cherry tree, a groundhog and his shadow, Ichabod Crane and the headless horseman, Honest Abe Lincoln, Jesse James, Johnny Appleseed, Judge Roy Bean and his pet bear, Kilroy, Billy the Kid, Molly Pitcher, John Henry, Paul Bunyan and his blue ox "Babe," Pecos Bill riding a mountain lion, Pocahontas & John Smith, Rip Van Winkle, Rosie the riveter, Two-Toe Tom the giant alligator, the unsinkable Mrs. Brown, Captain Kidd and his treasure, Jean Lafitte the world's busiest buccaneer, a yellow-eyed goat that sees red, and other exceptional Americans and their amazing animals. These stories are great for reading alone or aloud with adults or children. Author Charles Sullivan has been praised by *The New York Times:* "Sullivan writes with a relaxed, modern tone ('easy come, easy go,' as Jesse James used to say) but never slangy. Although he skillfully slips in details of history and geography, he also conveys a sense of spirit and energy."

Contact Information
Email the publisher: kezaco@earthlink.net. Telephone (415) 362-2262. Or fax (415) 474-4544.

Copyright & License Notices

Author's Bonus to the Reader

Included for you to read in this ebook *Santa Fe Voices* is a sample of nine stories, copyright 2012 by Charles Sullivan. These folk tales may provide additional perspectives on life in New Mexico and other parts of the great Southwest, past and present. To read more of Sullivan's stories about exceptional Americans and their amazing animals, look for his ebook *Uncle Sam's Family*.

CINDERELLA OF SANTA FE

Once upon a time there was a pretty girl named Gertrudes de Barcelo, who lived with her father and stepmother in the humblest of neighborhoods in Santa Fe, New Mexico. Gertrudes planned to become a princess, just as soon as she had saved enough money to leave home. This was no dream. Day or night, Gertrudes thought about taking the Trailways bus to Palm Beach, Florida, and marrying a prince! She had found magazine articles about Miami, Tucson, Lake Tahoe, and other resorts, but Palm Beach was the home of the young man who appealed to her most: Leland J. Costello, the Fourth. She cut out pictures of him and kept them in a scrapbook.

Falling asleep at night, Gertrudes imagined her first date with the prince she had chosen for herself. He was tall, gentle, handsome. A curly lock of black hair fell across his brown eyes, and he kept pushing it back. He'd wear a splendid blue blazer, or possibly a fancy uniform, and ask her politely if she could waltz. Of course she could! Gertrudes loved to dance, any step or any tempo. Together they would whirl across the shining floor of the palace ballroom, always in sync, just the two of them, while other couples looked on. But what would she be wearing?

"Wake up, Gertie!" her stepmother shouted. "It's one a.m., and time for you to go to work."

"But what would I be wearing?" Gertrudes repeated, still half asleep.

"The same things you always wear, my darling. Blue jeans, a blouse, and sandals."

Gertrudes washed herself, dressed swiftly, and hurried through the dark streets to the old-fashioned dance hall where she was employed, cleaning the bathrooms, sweeping up trash, waxing the wooden floor for tomorrow's customers.

Even at this late hour, there were still a few people dancing near the bandstand: girls she knew and officers from the military base nearby. As Gertrudes watched them, the manager of the dance hall approached her.

"I'm sorry, sir," she stammered. "I know I should be working, not just standing here. I'll stay later to make up for it."

"Relax a moment," the manager replied. "You know, Gertie, I've been thinking about you."

Gertrudes had heard this kind of talk from men before, and she waited silently for the rest of it. But the manager surprised her.

"You're a wonderful dancer," he smiled. "I've seen you waltzing around the floor with a mop in your arms, late at night, when nobody else was watching."

"I'm sorry," Gertrudes said. "It won't happen again."

"Oh, but it should happen," the manager insisted. "Don't you see? We need another girl around here. To dance with customers, I mean. Only to dance with them. Nothing personal, Gertrudes, if you understand me."

Gertrudes agreed to try it. The manager's wife would find her something to wear. And the pay would be twice as much as she was making now. Plus tips! She could buy some new clothes, and a bus ticket to Palm Beach that much sooner.

And dancing! Her thoughts were full of dancing as she did the chores, hour after hour, and trudged home at noon.

Too tired to be hungry, she ate some breakfast to please her adoring stepmother. Then she fell asleep and dreamed again of being the princess rescued by an elegant prince.

The next evening, Gertrudes changed into a red satin gown. It barely covered her shoulders, and she was embarrassed. But the manager's wife also gave her a lacy shawl to wear over it. Gertrudes entered the hall more excited than she had been in years.

Night after night, Gertrudes danced with men of every variety, including ranch hands, truck drivers, and military officers. Some of them were good-looking, a few could waltz, yet for her it was just another dance in the arms of a stranger: nothing magical about it. Gertrudes longed to hear the gentle voice of her charming prince, to float around the floor without having her feet stepped on! She was making plenty of money now. As she got closer to leaving her job in Santa Fe, however, the prince's palace in Palm Beach seemed farther and farther away.

Early one Saturday morning, as Gertrudes was getting ready to go home, she noticed a solitary figure at the far end of the hall, dancing with a mop as she used to do. She recognized Fernando, the shy young man who had been hired to take her place cleaning. Tall, black-haired, and barefoot, he moved so gracefully that Gertrudes waited for several minutes before she spoke.

"May I have this dance?"

Fernando looked at her with astonishment, suddenly awakened from his dreams by the voice of a real princess.

ELFREGO BACA THE FEARLESS DEPUTY

Back in the days when our "Wild West" truly was kind of wild, the men who served as deputy sheriffs could be tall, short, fat, skinny, young, old, brave, or maybe not so brave. Elfrego Baca, for instance, was young, short, and skinny: nothing much to look at. Elfrego kept his new deputy's badge brightly polished, however, and his Colt .44 revolvers polished as well. He wore two heavy gunbelts of extra ammunition crossed low on his hips, with the fancy leather holsters tied down like a gunfighter's.

But what could you tell from that? Elfrego might have been what he appeared to be: a tough young deputy, a deadly shot, ready to enforce the law no matter what. Or maybe he just wanted people to think so. In fact his real life was not very exciting.

After two years of uneventful service as a sheriff's only deputy, Elfrego had to accept the reality that there was very little crime in the town of Frisco, New Mexico, where he worked. His elderly boss, the sheriff, slept most of the day and visited the town's only saloon at night, making any arrests that were necessary. Elfrego was stuck with the boring jobs, such as guarding the few prisoners and fetching their meals, cleaning out cells, and doing the paperwork because his boss supposedly couldn't read or write.

Late one Saturday afternoon in March of 1884, Elfrego finished writing a report, closed the sheriff's large rolltop desk, and strolled down the main street of the town to see what was happening. Very little, as usual. Passing the saloon where his white-haired boss could be seen enjoying some liquid refreshment, Elfrego continued along the wooden sidewalk to the livery stable. He told the man who owned it that he would need to hire an extra horse on Monday.

"Where you goin', Deputy?"

"Sheriff's sending me over to Pasiente, to deliver a prisoner for trial next week."

Pasiente, slang for El Paso, was just a few miles away from Frisco, and that was where Federal judges held court for southern New Mexico as well as the northwest corner of Texas. Elfrego's prisoner, a Texan, had been in and out of the Frisco jail a dozen times before.

"What's he done this time?" asked the stable owner. "Mean, drunk and disorderly again?"

"No, worse than that," said Elfrego. "He chased a Hispanic girl into the barrio last night. Hurt her pretty bad. Then he beat up her kid brother, who was trying to stop him."

"Nobody told me," the man said.

Elfrego wasn't surprised. Even in a small town like Frisco, the Mexican neighborhood was like a distinct and separate world that most of the other residents didn't know much about.

Back in the office, with nothing to do, Elfrego looked at the latest bunch of WANTED posters. Some mighty bad characters, and some mighty big rewards being offered, but nothing connected with the town of Frisco. Just to keep his mind sharp, though, Elfrego made a list of names, and tried to memorize the faces that went with them.

"Hey, jailer," a voice growled from the row of cells behind him. Elfrego turned. It was the trouble-loving Texan that he had to take to El Paso next week.

"So you're awake," Elfrego responded. "What can I do for you?"

"Steak, fried eggs, and plenty of coffee," said the cowboy, whose name was Frank Magee. "And be darn quick about it! I'm hungry enough to eat the front half of a steer, horns and all."

"I'll bring you some food as soon as the sheriff gets back," said Elfrego.

Magee started cursing. Elfrego ignored him. He had no other prisoners to guard tonight, but now that this troublesome fellow was up and about, he didn't want to leave him alone, even in a locked jail.

"You can't keep me here like this," Magee growled. "I'm an American citizen, first class, and I know my rights."

"You'll appear before the judge in El Paso on Monday or Tuesday," Elfrego replied. "Until then you're staying right here. . . ."

"When I get my hands on you," Magee was roaring, "I'll. . . ."

"Partly for your own protection," Elfrego continued. "A few people in this town would like to have words with you."

"People, did you say, or Mexicans?" Magee sneered. "There's a mighty big difference where I come from."

"But maybe not such a very big difference where you're going," Elfrego said under his breath.

"What's that?" cried Magee, rattling the barred door of his cell. "Why you ornery little. . . ."

At this moment the fat old sheriff walked in, caught the tone of this conversation, burped a couple of times, and sat down at his desk.

"Go get some food for the prisoner," he told Elfrego, tossing him a silver dollar.

"And don't forget my coffee," Magee shouted after him.

Outside, Elfrego breathed deeply and leaned against the wall of the jail for a moment. It would be wrong to hit a prisoner, of course, but he had been tempted! He took another deep breath and looked around.

Sunset had streaked the western sky bloody red between adobe buildings. Though Frisco didn't have much to offer, it seemed a lot better than nothing on a Saturday night. The main street was busy now, with townspeople and cowboys from the nearby ranches, out looking for some kind of fun. As he walked towards the saloon to get a tray of food for the prisoner, Elfrego recognized most of the faces he saw. No, here were some strangers hitching their horses to the post in front of the bank, which was closed and dark. Ten or twelve of them. Dressed like ordinary cowboys. Texans, by the way they talked.

One of the strangers pulled a shotgun out of a saddlebag, and Elfrego instantly reached for his pistols; but a moment later the man put the weapon away, and crossed the street to the saloon with his companions. Elfrego relaxed, followed the strangers inside, and observed them from a distance as he waited for his take-out order to be filled. Everything was peaceful so far. Don't look for trouble, Elfrego told himself.

He bought a Mexican beer, Dos Equis, his favorite brand, and paid for it with small change. Sipping it slowly, he counted a dozen of those Texans, mostly taller than average, each wearing one or two gunbelts like his. They were talking loud and drinking fast. Apparently they had money. . . .

One of them turned towards Elfrego. This man looked like Frank Magee! Maybe a brother or a cousin of the prisoner. Maybe the Texans were going to try a jailbreak! Elfrego picked up the food he'd ordered, and hurried out into the dark street.

He found the sheriff asleep sitting up. Magee, the prisoner, was lying on his bunk with a hat over his eyes. Elfrego unlocked the cell with his right hand while holding the tray of food with his left. When the cell door was wide open,

Magee leaped up, grabbed Elfrego around the neck, over-powered him, and snatched one of his pistols, firing a wild shot into the floor. This awakened the sheriff, who reached under his coat for a gun as Magee fired again and killed him.

"Put your other pistol on the table there," Magee yelled at Elfrego, "or you're a dead man."

The young deputy did as he was told. Then Magee leaned forward to pick up his pistol, and Elfrego hit him smack in the face with a full pot of hot coffee. Magee fell to his knees, screaming. Elfrego took both guns away from him, and put steel handcuffs on his wrists, but Magee was too heavy to drag back into a cell. So the deputy used an-other pair of cuffs to fasten the prisoner's right arm to the heavy iron safe in which evidence was sometimes kept. Magee, moaning with pain, asked for some water. Elfrego pushed a bucket towards him with the handle of a broom.

"Use what's left in that," said Elfrego. Now his heart was beating rapidly like an Apache drum, but he knew what he had to do: lock the door of the jail, secure the windows, and start loading bullets into the Winchester rifles that the sher-iff had stored in a closet.

"You're wasting your time, little man," Magee snarled. "The whole front of this jail is going to blow wide open, just about an hour from now. And as for you, *chiquito*, you're going right ahead to meet your Maker, maybe five minutes after that!"

Elfrego didn't answer. He used wooden tables and chairs to barricade the windows and the door as best he could, and placed the loaded rifles where he could reach them in a hurry. Meanwhile, Magee was crouching behind the iron safe, as close to the floor as possible.

BAM! The front door of the jail, and part of the wall, ex-ploded into chunks of wood and metal. Elfrego felt something cut his cheek. Smoke filled the room. Bullets flew through the shattered window and the gaping doorway. Masked men could be seen dimly in the street, guns blazing.

"Now what, little fellow?" Magee sneered.

"Now I'm going to chase your friends away," Elfrego assured him.

"Fat chance!"

Firing through two broken windows, Elfrego cleared the street with rapid fire from two Winchester rifles, one after the other. Men cried out and scattered. Then he stood in the doorway of the jail with a third rifle, picking off the outlaws as they showed themselves to shoot at him. Gradually their guns were silenced.

Elfrego knew he had been nicked a couple of times, but not seriously hurt. After it was all over, he stepped outside, looked around, and said a brief prayer of thanks. The fierce gun battle had lasted only a short while, maybe twenty minutes at the most, yet the youthful deputy felt that it had changed the direction of his life in some important way.

Years later, while he was studying in Los Angeles to become a lawyer, Elfrego was asked about his famous gunfight back in Frisco, New Mexico. This eager man actually wanted his autograph!

"I heard it was maybe twenty or thirty to one against you," the man said. "I heard you killed more than half of them Texas cowboys before the rest of them gave up."

"Well, there weren't more than twelve to start with," Elfrego replied, "and I'd say I wounded three or four, maybe five, but I didn't kill anybody. I never wanted to kill anybody. To tell you the truth, I really wasn't that good of a shot, and my hand would usually shake when I pulled the trigger. But you know how Texans love to enlarge a story."

JUDGE ROY BEAN AND HIS PET BEAR

In the 1890s a short, nervous-looking Texan named Henry "Hank" Ketchum decided to try his hand at cattle rustling. He had been fairly honest up to that point, working at a general store in Del Rio, but the struggling store went out of business and Hank couldn't find another job, so he thought he would just steal a few head of cattle and sell them for whatever price he could get. Then maybe he'd use that money to move to Oklahoma and start over.

Hank saddled his broken-down horse one evening, and rode out across the prairie to the nearest ranch, figuring that the wealthy owners would never miss a little livestock on a moonless night. He swung his rope overhead, around and around in a big loop, as he had seen cowboys do in rodeos, and then flung it in the general direction of the nearest steer. Or what might have looked like a steer in the dark. Actually it was a sleepy horse belonging to the ranch foreman, who happened to be sitting on it at the time, taking his turn at guarding the herd. Hank's swirling rope hit the foreman right smack in the face, knocking his hat off and making him see stars for a moment.

"What in tarnation?" the foreman yelled. He raised his shotgun, squinted in Hank's direction, fired a couple of shots, and quickly put an end to Hank's brief career as a cattle rustler. Tied up loosely with his own rope and prodded by the ranch foreman, Hank was forced to walk the two miles back to town, hoping he could find a way out of the trouble he was in.

But the Texas laws about rustling cattle were generally clear and simple in those early days. They were especially clear and simple in that particular part of Texas, where a man known as "Judge" Roy Bean often decided who was guilty of what. Roy Bean was also in business as a saloonkeeper, but he had studied the law for a while, somewhere or other, and he had two thick law books that he used to quote or misquote from. Since there was no other legal authority for many miles around, lots of folks brought their legal issues to him for a decision.

Judge Bean's "courtroom" consisted of the rear area of his saloon, where a thick slab of blackjack oak rested on two empty barrels. He sat behind this "bench" with a glass of bourbon close to his left hand and a Remington .44 army revolver next to his right hand. When Hank Ketchum was brought before him and accused, the Judge had nothing better to do, so he listened attentively to every detail of the case, from both sides, and then made his decision.

"Guilty of cattle rustling as charged," he said. "Mister Ketchum, you are hereby fined five dollars cash for court costs, and sentenced to death by hanging. That's my ruling."

Judge Bean was just about to adjourn the court, when suddenly a better idea occurred to him.

"Hold on a minute," he told his helpers. "Bring the prisoner back here. A plea for clemency has been entered."

Hank stood anxiously before the Judge for a second time, wondering what was going to happen to him next.

"Mr. Ketchum, your sentence is hereby reduced to thirty days of animal husbandry," the Judge declared. Having no gavel, he banged the handle of his pistol down on the wooden slab, and that was that.

"Court adjourned!"

Hank didn't know just who or what clemency might be,

and he wasn't sure about animal husbandry, either. However it sounded a whole lot better than being hanged by the neck, so Hank politely thanked the Judge and followed him outdoors.

Behind the saloon a large brown bear lived alone, in what used to be a corral for the Judge's horses. Hank soon understood that he was going to be living there too. The bear came over to the gate, sniffed at Hank, and waited as the Judge locked Hank inside.

"This here is Lily, the light of my life," said the Judge. "Feed her and brush her coat for thirty days, sing her a song now and then, and your thirty days will be done before you can say skid-ee, skid-oo!"

Hank gradually adjusted to his new way of life, eating when Lily ate, sleeping when she slept, and singing her the songs he had learned as a drummer boy in the Army, such as "Yellow Rose of Texas" and "When Johnny Comes Marching Home." The big bear especially liked marching around and around the otherwise empty corral, following Hank as he sang.

After a month of this, Judge Bean was so pleased that he added thirty more days to the sentence, and Hank realized that he might be stuck there forever. The next moonless night, he climbed out of the corral to freedom. Lily followed him, naturally. The two of them walked away unchallenged, disappearing into the dark reaches of the Texas prairie as they headed for the distant hills. Lily found a cave of friendly bears living out there, and went no further, but Hank kept going for several more weeks, following old Indian trails until he stumbled into the unclaimed oil fields of Washington County, Oklahoma, and struck it rich.

PECOS BILL RIDES A MOUNTAIN LION

Bill Kimble left home at age eighteen, for one reason or another, and made his way to the well-known "Bar None" ranch in West Texas, near the Rio Grande River. He wanted to be a cowboy. He was possessed of enormous strength and determination, although he had no work experience to speak of.

"You can't hardly ride a horse. You've never roped a steer. You don't know one end of a branding iron from the other," said the hard-eyed cattleman who owned this sprawling ranch. "So what use are we supposed to make of you here?"

"I'll try anything," Bill replied. "Just give me a chance."

"Anything?" the rancher said doubtfully. "We'll have to see about that."

In exchange for room and board and a dollar a day in cash wages, Bill took the back-breaking job of hauling water from the Rio Grande to fill some shallow clay basins where thirsty steers could drink. There were dozens of these man-made basins scattered across the huge ranch, and Bill worked really hard from sunup to sundown to keep them full on hot summer days, using leaky wooden buckets. At first he tried to carry two or three full buckets with each hand, but he spilled too much water that way. One morning his boss, the ranch foreman, showed him a broken-down old wagon in the barn.

"You'll have to fix it up and pull it yourself," the boss said. "I've got no horses to spare for things like that."

Bill was somewhat scared of this boss, a mean little fellow who looked like a cactus with a mustache, so he didn't argue. He repaired the wagon with some pieces of wood, and made a harness of ropes to pull it with.

Things went better for a while. From week to week, however, Bill noticed that the level of water in the Rio Grande was lower and lower. It was getting harder and harder for him to fill his buckets, even out in the middle of the river. Finally he had to tell his boss the bad news: there was no more water to be had.

"Well, you'll just have to find water somewhere else," his boss replied, "if you want to keep on working here."

Bill didn't realize his boss might be asking too much of him. He went jogging that night, in a wide circle around the ranch, looking for ponds or streams to keep the cattle supplied with water until this dry spell was over. His search seemed hopeless: now even the smallest water holes were empty. At dawn he scanned the sky, but it was cloudless as usual. There might be no rain until the weather got cooler in the fall.

"What about the Pecos River?" his boss asked.

"Dry as a bone," said Bill.

"I heard there was water in it, further up," the boss insisted. "Go take another look."

Bill hastily finished his breakfast of steak and eggs, and hurried out the door. By noon he had reached the Pecos. He followed the dry, sandy bed of the river northward. After a few more miles he discovered some shallow puddles of water. . . not enough to fill many buckets, but surely better than nothing. . . and a tiny stream trickled down from one puddle to the next. Then some passing cowboys told him there was a lake, a pretty big one, in the hills farther north. Bill hurried back to the ranch and asked his boss if he could borrow a plow.

"For what?" the boss demanded. "You gonna be Farmer Bill now? I thought you was aiming to be a cowboy."

"I'll cut a channel up to that lake," Bill explained, "but first I'll dig out a pond at this end, so the water won't just run away when it gets down here."

Bill took off his shirt and boots, and started pushing the plow around the dry clay soil. He loved to work hard. He kept at it all day, without taking a break, despite the heat. By suppertime, when his boss and the other hands came riding in from the range, the hole for the new pond was half a mile across and forty feet deep.

"Not bad," his boss admitted. "I can see where you're trying to go with this. But it still don't have no water in it."

Early the next morning, Bill made an opening in the north side of his empty pond, and started cutting a channel to the north. He pushed his plow swiftly across miles of empty prairie, then up the dry riverbed of the Pecos towards the lake he'd heard about. Hour after hour, plowing through clay or sand or gravel, Bill kept on going. When he finally got to the lake, however, it was almost empty, and the many hoof-prints of cattle around the edges told him it must be heavily used.

"Got to go further," Bill thought.

As the moon rose he left the lake behind, following the dry riverbed, pushing steadily to the north with his plow. At dawn the next day he crossed into New Mexico, but there still wasn't enough water in the Pecos River to wet more than his bare feet. Somewhere in the hills between Santa Fe and Las Vegas, he found a bubbling spring where the river actually began, and there was nothing more to plow; he couldn't go any further.

That afternoon Bill sat beside his river, watching a shiny trickle of water coming out of the ground. Tired now, and

_____

73

more than a little hungry, he closed his eyes. As he slept the sky slowly darkened, and warm summer rain came pouring down, filling the narrow riverbed, overflowing the banks of the Pecos, soaking the dry land.

Bill woke up, saw what was happening, and laughed happily. At last his job was done!

"But I'm not going back to cattle-ranching in Texas any more," he decided. "No Sirree! I been there, I done that."

Reaching into a nearby cave, Bill pulled out a reluctant rattlesnake, made a loop of it, and roped a wet, bewildered mountain lion to ride on. Snake and lion soon understood who was in charge.

As the rain stopped, Bill dried himself with tumbleweed and moved out, eager for the adventures he knew he would find in the high desert west of the Pecos.

BLACK BART THE STAGECOACH ROBBER

A man who called himself "Charles E. Boles" taught school in a California mining town during the early 1870s, when gold could still be found by those willing to dig deep enough for it. Boles was a slim, quiet, neatly dressed individual who kept mostly to himself, yet every once in a while he surprised people with his big toothy smile and his wild, unexpected outbursts of humor.

He just loved to play practical jokes. Not on any of his students, but almost anybody else: another teacher, or a friend or acquaintance, sometimes even a total stranger. He always looked dignified and serious while he carefully prepared the surprise. Then, as his victim realized it must be a joke, Boles would burst into loud laughter, slapping his thighs, whooping and hollering like a man gone crazy.

One day his joking went too far. Boles was riding home after school, guiding his gray horse along a rough trail that crossed the main road, when he saw a red and yellow Wells Fargo stagecoach coming slowly up the mountain. He recognized the man who was driving, and thought it would be fun to scare him a little. So Boles hid his horse behind some mesquite shrubs, broke off a crooked stick to pretend he had a pistol, tied a bandana over his mouth for a mask, and stepped out into the road as the stage approached. It stopped abruptly.

"Throw down your moneybox!" Boles shouted.

The driver, surprised and frightened, did just that, and the heavy metal box burst open when it hit the ground beside the road, spilling out golden bars and several canvas sacks of gold dust. No telling how much all of this might be worth! As Boles stood there, forgetting to reveal who he was, the driver yelled at the horses and the stagecoach rolled away.

Bart started packing the gold back into the box, thinking he could catch up with the stagecoach and explain his joke to the driver and passengers. But then he thought some more. Even if he continued to teach school for many years, he couldn't earn nearly as much money as this treasure was worth right now; why not just keep it? Stealing was wrong, of course, but remaining poor didn't seem to be exactly the right idea either. Boles quickly stuffed the gold into his saddlebags and rode off, leaving the empty Wells Fargo box behind. Thus began his new and exciting career as a bandit.

When he got home to his rented wooden shanty, Boles did what a lot of people in those parts did: he pried up one of the floorboards to make a hiding place. Down there he placed one small sack of gold dust, an old watch that lacked a minute hand, and various other odds and ends of no great value. He was tempted to add some kind of a funny note for any robber who might come along, but then he supposed it might be better to leave well enough alone. The rest of the gold he buried out in the brush at several different locations, which he memorized before doing another thing.

During the next seven years, Charles Boles held up more than thirty Wells Fargo stagecoaches, mostly in California's mountainous "gold country" where he knew every turn of the roads. Some drivers were braver than others, some stages carried armed guards as well, but Boles always managed to take them by surprise, usually at a spot where the stage was going slowly, climbing a steep grade or starting to cross a stream. He never fired a shot, and never got caught. Well, almost never; detectives from Wells Fargo did catch up with him, but that was later on.

Compared to other outlaws, Boles was probably luckier and smarter than most. He planned every detail in advance, and was careful about disguising himself and hiding his tracks. But he could never resist a joke. After each robbery of a stagecoach, he would leave a humorous note in the empty moneybox. For example:

> "This is my way to get money and bread.
> When I have a chance, why should I refuse it?
> I'll not need either when I'm dead,
> And I only tax those who are able to lose it.

> "So blame me not for what I've done,
> I don't deserve your curses;
> And if for some cause I must be hung,
> Let it be for my verses."

Boles signed each of these poetic notes with a name that was also meant to be a joke, "Black Bart, the Po-8."

Not long after Black Bart the poet began holding up Wells Fargo stagecoaches, Mr. Charles E. Boles the schoolteacher quit his job and quickly disappeared from the mining community where he had been working. Coincidentally a prosperous and well-dressed gentleman who used the name "C. E. Bolton" arrived in San Francisco, and let it be known that his prosperity came from several goldmines up in the mountains, which he had to visit periodically. Nobody connected Bolton with Boles, or either one of those two with Black Bart, and it was only by chance that the poetry-writing bandit was finally caught. The vital clue to his identity was discovered because of the brave actions of a fifteen-year-old boy named Jimmy Roleri.

On a fine November day in 1883, near the Stanislaus River in California's central valley, Black Bart held up the stagecoach in which Jimmy Roleri was coming back from a visit to his grandparents. When Bart suddenly appeared out of nowhere, waving his gun, the driver threw down the moneybox without a fight, but this time it didn't break open right away.

Smash! Bart attacked the box, using the sledgehammer and chisel that he always carried with him just in case. Splintering the lid, he kicked it aside.

The box was partly full of gold, as usual, and Bart lost no time loading it into the saddlebags on his nearby horse. He needed only two or three minutes to do all of this. Then he put his usual note in the moneybox and climbed onto his horse.

When Jimmy Roleri realized what was happening, he slipped out the far side of the coach and crouched behind it, taking the new .22-caliber single-shot rifle he had been given for his birthday. Just as Black Bart was about to ride away, Jimmy aimed the rifle and fired his one shot.

Bart was hit in the arm or hand. He lost his black derby hat as he galloped off. And a detachable white cuff, spotted with blood, fell from the sleeve of his shirt.

At last the detectives who worked for Wells Fargo, led by an expert named James Hume, had a couple of clues to follow. The derby hat didn't help much, because they couldn't tell who might have owned it. But the shirt cuff, made of best white linen, had been marked "F.X.0.7" by a commercial laundry somewhere to identify a particular customer. Find that laundry and they would have their man!

More than three dozen Wells Fargo detectives spread out across the rugged landscape of the "gold country," looking for the laundry that had marked someone's shirt that way. No luck in the mining towns, where most people did their own washing, or did without. No luck in nearby cities such as Placerville or Sacramento, where the Chinese laundry workers always marked things in their own language.

So the detectives spread out further, some going as far as Las Vegas and Los Angeles. Finally, in San Francisco, the detective found a laundry that recognized the "F.X.0.7" mark and identified their customer: Mr. C. E. Bolton, who resided at an elegant private hotel, the Webb House, not far away.

The rest was easy. Having stationed several of his best men along the hallway and downstairs beneath the windows, chief detective Hume knocked on the door of Bolton's hotel suite, carrying a bundle of clean shirts from the laundry, as though he were making a delivery. When Bolton started to pay him, Hume interrupted.

"I think this may also be yours, Bart."

Hume handed him the blood-spotted shirt cuff that had led the detectives to him. Bart was surprised of course, and scared; but he had to laugh too, because this time the joke was on him.

Bolton/Bart/Boles served six years in San Quentin prison for armed robbery. That brought an end to his poetry, but his story wasn't quite finished. Indeed, there are several different accounts of what Black Bart did in his later years. Let's pick one and follow it to the end.

Soon after Bart was released from prison, a masked bandit began holding up the few Wells Fargo stagecoaches that still carried gold down from the mines in the mountains. Each time this robber took the stage drivers by surprise, never firing a shot, and each time he managed to get away. Though the shipments were much lighter and less frequent than they had been before, there was still enough gold in the moneyboxes for a patient, experienced bandit to make a living.

No funny notes were left in the boxes now, and no more poetry, but the Wells Fargo detectives were pretty sure they knew who was doing these robberies. So they searched for him again in San Francisco, found him pretty easily, and had a friendly chat. Bart told them he wasn't getting any younger. Actually he would like to retire from this line of work, if he could be assured of enough money to live on.

"How about a monthly payment from the company?" he asked.

Black Bart may have meant this as a joke, but the detectives took it seriously. Three days later, Wells Fargo decided to pay him a comfortable little pension each month for the rest of his life, if he would solemnly promise to stop robbing them. Bart gave his word, shook hands on the deal, and that was the end of his story.

SWEET BETSEY FROM PIKE

Elizabeth Curry was the prettiest girl in Pike County, Missouri, although she didn't want to be. She wore nice dresses, proper shoes, and hair ribbons because she had to: going to school, going to church, serving tea or orange punch to her parents' guests at home, visiting relatives in St. Louis or Columbia. Whenever she could get free for a while, even if it was just an hour or so in the afternoon, she would quickly change into her faded blue jeans, an old buckskin shirt, and her treasured Indian moccasins. Then she'd put on a well-worn cowboy hat to hide the golden glory of her long hair, as she tried to sneak out of the house.

"Elizabeth!" her exasperated mother would plead with her. "Now just you wait a minute, young lady! Where do you think you'll be going in those outlandish clothes? Are you meeting someone? I don't know what's to become of you, I'm sure."

Betsey didn't know what was to become of her, either, but she usually made some acceptable excuse and slipped through the doorway before her mother could stop her. Outside she'd head for the hill behind the house, where she could gaze in all directions, or she'd walk to the livery stable where she was sometimes allowed to exercise horses. Today she felt like doing both: borrowing a horse, riding it to the very top of her hill, choosing a new destination, and galloping away. But where to? Where should she go? That was always the problem.

Down at the livery stable, Betsey got a surprise. Her best friend, a young man by the name of Ike Henderson, was selling both of his riding horses.

"Headin' to California," Ike explained. Goin' to buy a wagon and two yoke of oxen, and join this Gold Rush that everybody's been talkin' about."

He was a big, gentle fellow, a few years older than Betsey, with a sweet disposition and something carefree about him, despite his serious expression at the moment.

"You're not really leaving without me, are you?" cried Betsey. "My father says it's only Fool's Gold, as like as not."

For nearly an hour she tried to talk Ike out of going, but his mind was already made up. He had sold most of his belongings, and he would be joining up with a wagon train tomorrow. Betsey finally said good-bye to him and walked slowly homeward, feeling miserable for the first time in her life. She ate no supper and avoided her parents' eyes while she pondered what to do.

The next morning it was Betsey who surprised Ike, climbing aboard his wagon as he was about to hit the trail with the others.

"Don't ask," she said firmly. "I'm eighteen years old, I know what I'm doing, and I am going with you."

At first it was a great adventure for both of them, learning to drive the oxen, cooking their meals in the open, sleeping at the opposite ends of the wagon or out under the stars. Ike's old yellow dog slept between them, his spotted hog kept watch for them all night, and his Shanghai rooster woke them every morning at dawn.

After three or four weeks, however, they were getting tired of traveling. The wagon train creaked along so slowly, day after day, and there was little to discuss with people in other wagons except the weather or, of course, the distant prospect of gold. This seemed like anything but an adventure! Kansas was even flatter than Missouri; when Ike's old yellow dog ran away one afternoon, they could see the dust it raised for miles.

"Dog gone," said Ike with a forced smile, trying to make light of their loss.

Up through the Colorado foothills they toiled, and into the Rocky Mountains, where Ike traded his rooster for a well-used guitar and some lessons. To pass the time away, as they rode along in the wagon, he began writing a song:

"Did you ever hear of Sweet Betsey from Pike? She crossed the wide prairies with her HUM-HUM Ike. . . ."

Betsey looked curiously at Ike, pulled off her floppy sunbonnet, and shook out her thick golden hair.

"What's HUM-HUM?" she asked.

"Whatever you say it is," Ike replied, blushing.

So they were married near Salt Lake City, Utah, by a Mormon preacher, and Betsey continued the endless journey westward with her new husband. After rafting across the wide Platte River, they had to drop out of the wagon train when they lost a wheel. They sold their four oxen to buy supplies. They talked about what to do next.

"Ike," said Betsey, "you and I have found something much more precious than gold. Do we have to walk all the way to California to prove it?"

"No, Betsey, I guess not," her loving husband Ike replied.

They settled near Las Vegas and started a livery stable, which turned out to be quite successful. They enjoyed every moment of their busy life together. And a golden-haired daughter, born to them the following year, soon became known as the prettiest girl in all of Nevada, though she didn't want to be.

FUR-BEARING TROUT

A lot of people go looking for gold, and some of them find it, but some others don't; they have to settle for different things, such as the lead that was accidentally discovered among the hills of Colorado in 1877. There a group of would-be gold miners abruptly decided to become miners of lead instead; so they staked the necessary claims, named their new community "The City of Leadville," bought two wagons full of tools, worked hard, and made a decent living for several years.

Lead had all sorts of industrial uses in those early days, including pipes and window-frames and certain kinds of paint, not to mention the bullets that some people liked to fire out of their six-shooters and rifles in large quantities. Therefore the miners were usually able to sell every ounce of ore they could dig from the earth.

Things were going pretty well until the lead miners got word that twenty-four young ladies from Chicago were going to put on a spectacular show of singing, dancing, and acrobatic exercises at a theatre in Denver the following month. *"For Two Days Only,"* the notice said. *"Single Tickets $5.00 Each, Box Seats $10.00 Per Head. Free Admission If Bald!"*

Denver was only ninety miles away, and most of the miners hadn't seen a pretty girl in two or three years, so they decided to close down their mine for a week or so, and have some fun. But to do it properly, they needed some "citified" clothes to dress up in. And free admission if bald;

they liked the idea of saving money by getting rid of their hair. But how?

This problem was solved the following day, when a traveling salesman arrived at the mining camp. His wagon was loaded with boxes and trunks. He displayed a full range of gents' finery, ranging from shiny green suits and fancy yellow shoes to red silk neckties and English mustache wax. He also offered a mysterious liquid called "Patented Hair Subtractor" which was guaranteed to make people bald, for two dollars a bottle. None of the miners had ever paid more than a dollar-fifty for anything that came in a bottle, and they were hesitant.

"Sure it's high-priced," the fast-talking salesman agreed. "But look at it this way: here is the only patented product that will take hair off and keep it off, painlessly and permanently. Or else you get every penny of your money back."

Each of the lead miners bought some of this liquid, used it, lost their hair, and rode into Denver a month later, wearing their new clothes. They found half a dozen busy theatres, and quite a few women who might have been experts at song, dance, or even acrobatics, but not the special young ladies they were looking for. Disappointed, they rode all the way back to Leadville in gloomy silence. And their gloom deepened when they found that a safe containing most of the lead mine's profits had been stolen in their absence.

It took the lead miners nearly a year of extra-hard work to earn back the money they had lost as a result of clever deception and downright theft. During this difficult time, they experimented with various ointments and other remedies that promised to restore their hair, but none of those concoctions did any good at all.

Then one of the miners, Marcus Galena, had to travel home to Chicago because his widowed mother was seriously ill. There he happened to hear about a new "scientific" formula that had supposedly grown hair on the head of a bald gorilla at the Lincoln Park Zoo. It was called Hairzup, and it was mighty expensive, twenty-five dollars per gallon.

Now Marcus had no desire to be as hairy as a gorilla. However he asked people if they had heard anything about Hairzup, and he was taken to see an elderly man who happened to live near the zoo. This man had been bald most of his life. Now his hair hung down to his shoulders, and covered his face and hands. So this Hairzup worked, apparently, whatever its ingredients might be.

Marcus assumed that the other miners would be eager to buy some of this product when they heard about it. So he found the warehouse where it was sold, counted out a hundred silver dollars for four gallons, and started the long journey back to Leadville.

After leaving the train in Denver, Marcus rode through the rolling hills with four big glass jugs of Hairzup tied behind his saddle. He was more than halfway to camp when the horse's foot slipped on a crude log bridge crossing the Tarryall River. Two of the jugs got loose and fell, breaking on the rocks below and spilling their contents into the stream. But there were still two gallons left.

"You try it first," the other miners insisted. "If it works for you, maybe we'll use it too."

Marcus followed the printed instructions exactly, putting Hairzup on his bald head every eight hours, and wearing his hat day and night in order to keep the results a secret. The truth is that nothing much happened. But the other miners still avoided him, and he started feeling lonely. So on a bright Saturday morning in May he got dressed up in his shiny green "city" suit and rode off towards Denver to visit a woman with whom he had been exchanging postcards for the past year or more. As he crossed the Tarryall River he looked down, stopped, and got off his horse. The water was full of strange fish. Trout they looked like, sort of, but trout covered with thick black fur. . . .

After staring at these fish for a few moments, Marcus got an idea. No more of this lead mining for him! Instead, he staked his own property claim to 160 acres of land along both sides of the river, put up some tents and one-room cabins among the pine trees, and advertised in the biggest Eastern newspapers.

Fishermen, hunters, and just plain curiosity-seekers came from far and wide to try their luck fishing for "Fur-Bearing Trout." They caught quite a few of them, year after year, but the furry fish just kept on multiplying, and Marcus Galena just kept on making money. Presently he had a comfortable house built for himself among the bare boulders on nearby Bald Mountain. He persuaded the lady from Denver to marry him and live there, except for occasional trips to New York, San Francisco, and other places where they found exciting ways to spend his fortune.

And Marcus often smiled to himself from then on, pleased as he could be with the various twists and turns of his life, though he never did grow much hair.

Story from *Uncle Sam's Family,* copyright 2012 by Charles Sullivan

— ✷ —

JESSE JAMES OUTSMARTED

One of the exceptional things about Jesse James, the fast-moving man who robbed so many banks and trains during the 1870s, was that he usually didn't know what to do with his share of the money. He bought good horses for himself and kept a few dollars to live on, but he gave a lot away. "Easy come, easy go," Jesse used to say.

It surely was easy to get money, as the James gang became widely known and feared in Missouri, Kansas, Arkansas, and beyond. And it was easy to get rid of the money, too, when Jesse began helping those in need. Widows and orphans, for instance. And small farmers down on their luck. And army veterans who couldn't find work. To most of them, Jesse James seemed more like a hero than a thief; they wouldn't listen to anything said against him.

Out of all those people, Jesse never forgot a woman he met in October 1871, just after he and his brother Frank held up the railroad freight office in Fayetteville, Arkansas. The James boys got away with nearly five hundred dollars in paper money and coins. As they were riding out of town, with nobody pursuing them, Jesse remarked that it would be nice to stop and have a hot meal somewhere. Frank agreed. They swung away from the main road, onto an inviting trail that led back among the low green hills, and soon they came to a tidy-looking farm with smoke rising from the chimney of the house.

Jesse knocked. Presently a woman came to answer the door, holding a handkerchief to her face.

"What is it?"

The brothers introduced themselves. As Jesse hastily explained that they just wanted a home-cooked meal, and they would pay her well for it, Frank James studied the woman carefully. Tall, slender, wearing a shapeless black dress. Dark hair with streaks of gray. She didn't seem all that old, but her cheeks were wet as though she had been crying.

"Is something the matter, Ma'am?" Frank asked.

"My husband was killed in the war. I haven't been able to collect the money he had coming. Now it's just me and my two children, Stevie and Sue. . . they're at the school down the road. . . I've managed to keep this farm going, but now I've fallen behind with the mortgage payments. So the banker is coming out here at three o'clock this afternoon, and I haven't got enough to pay what I owe!"

She started to weep again, while the James brothers shifted their feet uncomfortably.

"Ma'am, how much do you owe the bank?" Jesse asked.

"All told? Four hundred dollars would do it. I could pay off that mortgage and burn it in the stove, once and for all. But I haven't got but fifty-two dollars saved up."

Jesse had more than enough money with him, so he offered to lend the widow the full amount she needed.

"And don't you worry about paying me right away," he added. "I'll come back this way next year, maybe, and that'll be soon enough."

After hearing Jesse's words, the widow perked up quite a bit. She fixed them a hearty lunch of corn bread and hot pea soup with plenty of ham scraps. It felt good to relax for a while, and they were in no hurry to leave. No hurry at all.

"Nothin' beats home cooking," Frank remarked.

"You can say that again," Jesse replied.

As she poured him a second cup of strong hot coffee, the widow's hand accidentally brushed his arm. Jesse was briefly struck by the thought that a man could do a lot worse for himself than this. But soon his restless spirit took over again; he got up from the table abruptly.

While Frank saddled their horses, Jesse insisted on paying the widow ten dollars for their meal, in addition to the loan of four hundred dollars, and the widow accepted. She stood in the doorway as they left, smiling through her tears.

Shortly after three o'clock that afternoon, Jesse and Frank took the dark-suited banker by surprise as he rode along the trail coming from the widow's farmhouse. The brothers had a simple plan: to rob him of the four hundred dollars they had loaned the widow to pay off her mortgage. That way, they figured, she would own her farm free and clear, so she wouldn't have to repay them anything, and they would be getting their money back to spend or to give away again.

The banker climbed slowly down off of his horse. Sure enough, there was a flat briefcase strapped behind the saddle, but it was empty.

"Where's your money?" Jesse demanded.

The banker twitched his thin black mustache.

"I just spent my money buying a farm back there. If you'll allow me to reach into my coat pocket, I'll show you the deed for the property."

"You mean there wasn't any mortgage on the place?" Frank blurted out.

"None that I'm aware of," the banker replied.

When Jesse and Frank got back to the farmhouse, it was deserted. The kitchen floor had been neatly swept, the dishes were drying beside the sink, and there was a piece of paper on the table, weighted down by one silver dollar.

"Received of Jesse James," the paper said, "Four Hundred & Nine Dollars & No Sense. Signed, Mary Witter. Let this be a lesson to you."

Jesse couldn't see exactly what the lesson was supposed to be, but he thought about that woman for years afterwards, until he got too busy doing other things.

WIND-WAGON THOMAS

Thomas O'Bannion was a saltwater sailor from Ireland, like
his father and grandfather before him. He loved the bound-
less freedom of the ocean, the sky, the winds; it was hard for
Thomas when his ship finally reached its destination, where
he had to go ashore while cargo was unloaded, repairs
made, and supplies carried aboard for the next voyage.

Walking aimlessly through the crowded streets of Liver-
pool or Hong Kong, Oakland or Valparaiso, he felt little in-
terest in what he saw, and he could hardly wait to escape
the limited horizons of city life.

But one day in New Orleans, he happened to meet anoth-
er young man, as bright and adventurous as Thomas himself,
who talked enthusiastically about wanting to build a lot of
"flatboats." They were small wooden barges, pulled by mules
or pushed by men with long poles, that were just right for
inland waters such as the shallow western rivers that feed into
the Mississippi. This young man, by the name of Leo Schultz,
was looking for a partner to help him get rich.

"We'll put wheels on flatboats," he declared, "so they
can be used as wagons as well, and then we'll sell them to all
those Easterners who are so darn eager to go west." This
was right after the beginning of the "gold rush" of the 1850s,
when people were heading for California by ship, wagon,
horseback, or on foot.

"When they get there," Leo continued, "they can take
the flatboats apart and use the wood for houses."

He filled in the rest of his plan so confidently that Thomas agreed to join him in this venture, even if it meant turning away from the sea for a month or two.

The next morning, Thomas and his partner caught the stagecoach for Kansas, where they could build some flatboat wagons and sell them to Easterners crossing the Missouri River. As they traveled farther into the open country, Thomas was surprised to find that he was starting to like it. Later, when he could see vast stretches of prairie ahead, with the wind making waves through the grass, he felt as though he had almost gone back to sea. Not so bad here after all!

At a town called Westport Landing, Kansas, Thomas and his partner bought lumber and wagon wheels. Neither of them knew much about doing carpentry, but their design seemed simple enough: a flat, rectangular box made of sturdy wooden planks resting on two long beams. The hardest part was attaching the wheels so that they could turn freely without coming loose. Thomas tried to do it with bits of rope, which didn't work.

"Why don't we just give people the four wheels," Leo said impatiently, "and let them figure it out?"

Then along came someone from Charleston, South Carolina, who showed them how to carve wooden axles for the wheels. Problem solved. Soon they had four completed, and their first "flatboat wagon" was ready to sell.

Thomas and Leo put up a sign on the far side of the river, where the overland trail to the west began at the water's edge, and waited for customers. A few people stopped to look, but nobody wanted to buy. They lowered the price, and lowered it again. Still no sale. The two young partners were getting discouraged.

"I like your basic idea," one man said, "but I just can't afford it. You know, the cost of horses and mules is sky-high right now, and it would take at least two of them to pull that thing."

So Thomas and Leo reluctantly decided to go out of business. All they had to do was remove the wheels from their flatboat wagon, find a suitable cargo, and float it down the river to New Orleans. There they could deliver the cargo, sell the flatboat, and maybe the wheels, and Thomas could go back to sea.

At the very last minute, however, standing near the river with a brisk breeze blowing, Thomas had a better idea.

"We don't need horses or mules to pull this thing," he said. "All we have to do is add a mast and a sail."

Leo was doubtful, but Thomas persuaded him to try it. With the last of their money, they bought a small oak tree and trimmed it for the mast, a smaller one for a boom, and several white canvas tents from which they could stitch together one sail. Then all they had to do was add some ropes for the rigging, and a lot of heavy stones for ballast, and the world's first "windwagon" was ready to go!

Thomas and his partner jumped aboard, hoisted the new sail, and caught an evening breeze blowing west from the river. Once they were clear of the willow trees along the riverbank, the windwagon gained speed, and soon they were racing across the smooth, flat, seemingly endless prairie towards the setting sun. Thomas was so excited that he completely forgot about trying to steer the windwagon or slow it down. Straight as the truest seabird they flew with the wind from the east, hour after hour, until at last their wagon crashed into the purple foothills of the Rocky Mountains, more than a thousand miles from their starting point. From there they decided to walk the rest of the way to California, and they never came back.

YOUR TURN TO YIP, HOWL, AND BARK
about Santa Fe Voices...

If you like this book, please tell people
about it. Then get to your bookstore
and write a Customer Review.
Thank you!

www.ingramcontent.com/pod-product-compliance
Lightning Source LLC
Chambersburg PA
CBHW020625130626
46552CB00003B/1098